-5

# The Miracle of the First Poinsettia
## A Mexican Christmas Story

To my dear parents, Helen and Abe Fleischer, with happy memories
of our sunny days in Mexico together — J. O.

To Emiliano Zapata and Pancho Villa — F. N.

Barefoot Books
124 Walcot Street
Bath, BA1 5BG

First published in Great Britain in 2003 by Barefoot Books Ltd. This paperback edition published in 2004

This book was typeset in 15.5/18pt Granjon
The illustrations were prepared in watercolours, coloured pencils, wax and oil pastels on Fabriano paper

Graphic design by Glynis Edwards, Bath
Colour separation by Bright Arts, Singapore
Printed and bound in Singapore by Tien Wah Press Pte Ltd

This book has been printed on 100% acid-free paper

ISBN 1-84148-364-8

British Cataloguing-in-Publication Data: a catalogue record
for this book is available from the British Library
1 3 5 7 9 8 6 4 2

# The Miracle of the First Poinsettia
## A Mexican Christmas Story

Written by **Joanne Oppenheim**

Illustrated by **Fabian Negrin**

**Barefoot Books**
*Celebrating Art and Story*

High in the mountains of Mexico daylight was beginning to fade. Soon it would be la Noche Buena, Christmas Eve. In the market Juanita wondered which piñata she would buy for her little brothers — if only she had the pesos to spend.

For most children it was a happy time. But not for Juanita, not this year. Papa had lost his job and they had no extra pesos for toys or sweets.

Señor Rojo waved to Juanita in the market-place. Maybe she could cut and tie strings for the marionettes that he sold — to earn extra coins for her family!

'Not today, Nita. I'm closing soon for la Navidad! This is for you, Nita.'

Señor Rojo gave Juanita a little sack of galletas, sweet biscuits. '¡Feliz Navidad, Nita!'

'¡Gracias, señor Rojo! ¡Gracias!'

Walking through the market, Juanita admired the towers of fruits. They looked delicious. How she wished she could take a small basket of bright red berries to place at the altar for the Baby Jesus, just as she had last year.

She wondered how much it would cost for just one little basket. '¿Cuánto es?' she asked, putting her hand out.

But señora Martínez seemed to misunderstand. 'No beggars here!' she scolded Juanita. '¡Vete! ¡Anda! ¡Largo de aquí!'

Juanita ran away. Why would the señora call her that? She was no beggar. She just wanted to buy presents for her family, and one small gift to take to the church, as the other children would that night.

Darkness was falling as Juanita hurried home. She was still trying to think of something she could take to the Baby Jesus. She had the galletas that señor Rojo had given her, but those were for her little brothers. Maybe she could make a small gift. But what?

Not far from her house Juanita's friends Margarita and Ana called to her. 'Nita! We have been looking for you! Come with us!'

Juanita always loved going singing with her friends. Every night for the nine nights before Christmas, families and friends went from house to house singing songs and then gathering together for las posadas — joyous fiestas to celebrate the coming of la Noche Buena. These were always the happiest nights of the year!

'Come on, Nita, come with us for the last posada!'
'I can't,' said Juanita. 'Mama needs my help.'
'Will you come to church with us later?' asked Ana.
'I have no gift to bring,' she answered.
'That doesn't matter!' said Margarita.

But it did matter to Juanita. How could she go to the church when all her friends were bringing gifts to the Baby Jesus and she had none?

That night there was no posada at Juanita's house. Together her family ate a simple meal of tortillas and beans with rice. Juanita gave the little ones the biscuits señor Rojo had given to her.

'Next year,' said Papa, 'I will have a new job and we will make a real party, a posada with a piñata and feast here in our little house!'

Papa took down his guitar and sang with Mama, Nita and her little brothers, Manuel and Pepito.

An hour before midnight, when the moon had risen in the sky, the old bells began to chime in the church tower.

'Come, Nita! It is time for church,' said Mama.

'No, I can't go,' answered Juanita.

Mama took Juanita's face in her hands. 'What is wrong?'

'I am not going.' Juanita felt the tears coming. 'I have no gifts. None for you or Papa or my brothers. And I have nothing to take to the Baby Jesus.'

'Ah, mi hija, you give gifts all the time. You gave galletas to your brothers. You sang songs for Papa. You bring such joy. To us, you are a gift!'

'But what about a gift for the Baby Jesus?'

'Ah, Nita-sita,' said Mama, 'there are no greater gifts than the ones you bring in your heart.'

From all over the village people made their way to the church. Juanita followed her parents who carried the little ones inside. But at the doorway Juanita stopped. She did not go in. How could she go into the church with nothing — not even a candle to place at the altar?

J uanita hid in the shadows outside the old church.
The tall doors were opened wide, and the music
of the mariachi band with brassy trumpets,
strumming guitars and joyous singers filled the night.

'*A la ru-ru-ru, niño chiquito,*
*Duérmase ya mi Jesusito.*'

Juanita hummed along as the mariachis sang an
old lullaby…

'*A la ru-ru-ru, my lovely Jesus,*
*In sweetest slumber now rest, my dearest.*'

Juanita could not hold her tears back any longer.
How she longed for everything to be as it had been
— when Papa was doing well and Christmas was
filled with joy!

'Juanita,' a sweet voice whispered.

Juanita looked behind her. She did not see anyone.

'Juanita,' the voice whispered again. 'Do you see the green leaves growing all around my wings?

Wings? Juanita looked around. The only wings she saw were on a little stone angel nestled among some weeds. Could a statue speak? How could that be? But it *must* have spoken!

'Pick the leaves, Juanita, and take them into the church,' said the angel.

J uanita was frightened and confused. She wondered how she could take such plain weeds to the Baby Jesus.

'Don't be afraid, Juanita,' the angel spoke again. It was as if she knew what Juanita was thinking. 'And don't worry about how the weeds look to you. To the Baby Jesus they will not look like weeds. He will know they are a gift from your heart!'

Juanita pulled at the tall, straggly leaves that grew around the little statue. She pulled and pulled until her arms were filled with a huge bunch of leafy green stalks.

At midnight, as Juanita walked into the church, she became very nervous. What would people say when they saw what she was bringing to the Baby Jesus? She was afraid to look to her left or right. Looking straight ahead, she could see the flickering light of hundreds of candles at the altar.

As Juanita made her way down the aisle of the crowded church she heard someone say, '¡Qué hermosa! How beautiful!' Another person whispered, '¡Qué linda!' To Juanita's surprise no one looked angry or upset. Why was everyone smiling at her?

It was then that Juanita realised that the armful of weeds she was carrying had been miraculously transformed into the most beautiful star-shaped scarlet-red flowers that she had ever seen.

She knew as she knelt and placed the glorious red flowers in front of the Baby Jesus that it was true. A gift from the heart is the best gift of all.

'Feliz Navidad, niño chiquito, Jesusito,' she whispered. 'Happy birthday.'

ever before had anyone seen such splendid flowers! The Mexicans called them 'Flores de la Noche Buena'.

Many people now call these flowers poinsettias.

They decorate homes and churches all over the world at Christmas time.

In Mexico they are so plentiful they still grow like weeds.

They brighten gardens and remind us of the hope, the joy and the miracle of Christmas!

# Author's Note

I came upon this story more than ten years ago while researching a book on how Christmas is celebrated around the world. The story was told in just three sentences, yet for me it brought a flood of ideas and memories.

For fifteen years my parents spent their winters in Mexico. Their home in Cuernavaca had a garden filled with bougainvillea climbing on the walls, lemon trees heavy with fruit, and a border of red poinsettias. They did indeed grow like weeds! I was lucky enough to visit my parents many times, but the most memorable trip was a Christmas holiday we spent together. Mexico City was like a fairyland with festive lights on every street and markets full of gifts. It was during the time of las posadas, and we could hear children singing as they went from house to house. These posadas are a part of a Mexican tradition that celebrates Mary and Joseph's journey to Bethlehem.

But the great highlight of that holiday trip was attending Midnight Mass in the cathedral in Cuernavaca where the joyous music is traditionally sung by the mariachis. In my mind's eye, I can still see the lights of the candles dancing and hear the sweet sound of the music as the people welcomed la Noche Buena.

In my research I have found many versions of this story. Sometimes the child is a boy — sometimes a girl. It is always a little different, yet the same. That is what keeps folktales alive — telling them and retelling them in different ways. Perhaps the reason this story lives on is because it is a miracle story that reminds us of the true spirit of giving. To me, it seems so fitting at Christmas and the season of miracles.

*Joanne Oppenheim*
*New York 2003*

# El rorro

## The Babe

A traditional Mexican carol sung by the mariachis at Christmas time

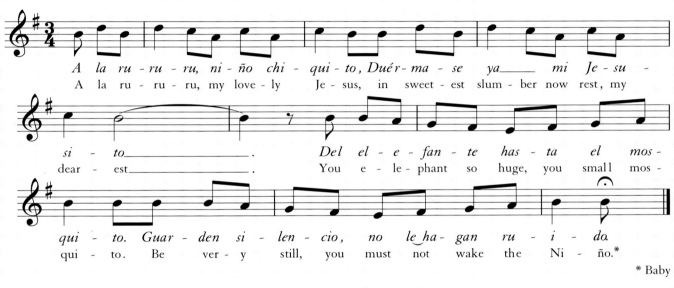

*A la ru - ru - ru, ni - ño chi - qui - to, Duér - ma - se ya___ mi Je - su -*
A la ru - ru - ru, my love - ly Je - sus, in sweet - est slum - ber now rest, my

*si - to___.* *Del el - e - fan - te has - ta el mos -*
dear - est___. You e - le - phant so huge, you small mos -

*qui - to. Guar - den si - len - cio, no le_ha - gan ru - i - do.*
qui - to. Be ver - y still, you must not wake the Ni - ño.*

\* Baby

2. *Noche venturosa, noche de alegría.*
   *Bendita la dulce, divina María.*
   Refrain

3. *Coros celestiales, con su dulce acento,*
   *Canten la ventura de este nacimiento.*
   Refrain

2. O night of glory, night of jubilation,
   So richly blest by Mary, Queen of Heaven.
   Refrain

3. Such heav'nly voices in sweet accents singing,
   The glorious tidings of His birth are bringing!
   Refrain

# Glossary

**¡Anda!** [*ahn-dah'*] Get going!

**¿Cuánto?** [*kuan'-toh*] How much?

**Feliz Navidad** [*feh-lees' nah-vee-dahd'*] Merry Christmas

**galletas** [*gah-yeh'-tahs*] biscuits

**gracias** [*grah'-see-ahs*] thank you

**¡Largo de aquí!** [*lar'-goh deh ah-kee'*] Get away from here!

**mariachi** [*mar-ee-ah'-chee*] a traditional Mexican band

**mi hija** [*mee ee'-hah*] my daughter

**Navidad** [*nah-vee-dahd'*] Christmas

**niño chiquito** [*nee'-nyoh chee-kee'-toh*] little one / young boy

**Noche Buena** [*noh'-cheh boo-eh'-nah*] Christmas Eve

**pesos** [*peh'-sos*] Mexican money

**piñata** [*peen-yah'-tah*] a papier mâché figure filled with sweets

**posadas** [*po-sah'-dahs*] celebrations that commemorate Mary and Joseph's
   journey from Nazareth to Bethlehem in search of shelter

**¡Qué hermosa!** [*keh er'-moh-sah*] How beautiful!

**¡Qué linda!** [*keh leen'-dah*] How pretty!

**señor** [*seh-nyohr'*] Sir

**señora** [*seh-nyohr'-a*] Madame

**tortillas** [*tor-tee'-yas*] thin pancakes made from cornmeal or wheat flour

**¡Vete!** [*veh'-teh*] Go away!